First published in Belgium and Holland by Clavis Uitgeverij, Hasselt – Amsterdam, 2014
Copyright © 2014, Clavis Uitgeverij

English translation from the Dutch by Clavis Publishing Inc. New York
Copyright © 2015 for the English language edition: Clavis Publishing Inc. New York

Visit us on the web at www.clavisbooks.com

Quiet Koala Noisy Monkey - a book of jungle opposites written and illustrated by Liesbet Slegers
Original title: *Lief en stoer in de jungle*
Translated from the Dutch by Clavis Publishing

ISBN 978-1-60537-237-2

This book was printed in June 2015 at Wai Man Book Binding (China) Ltd. Flat A, 9/F., Phase 1,
Kwun Tong Industrial Centre, 472-484 Kwun Tong Road, Kwun Tong, Kowloon, H.K.

First Edition
10 9 8 7 6 5 4 3 2 1

Quiet Koala

Noisy Monkey

a book of jungle opposites

Clavis

NEW YORK

Liesbet Slegers

Hello Zebra,
your stripes are
black and white.

Hello there, Parrot,
your feathers are
multi-colored.

Hey, Elephant and Frog,
you are both totally
dry.

Hello Koala, you're **sleepy** and **quiet** on your branch.

Hi Monkey, you are **active** and **noisy**.

Go ahead
and jump around, Lion!
It's **daytime**.

And now it's **nighttime.**
Have a good sleep.

Hi Crocodile, are you sitting there **alone**?

Aha, there are your friends.
Now, you are playing together.

Giraffe, your neck is so
short.
And where is the rest
of your body, Snake?

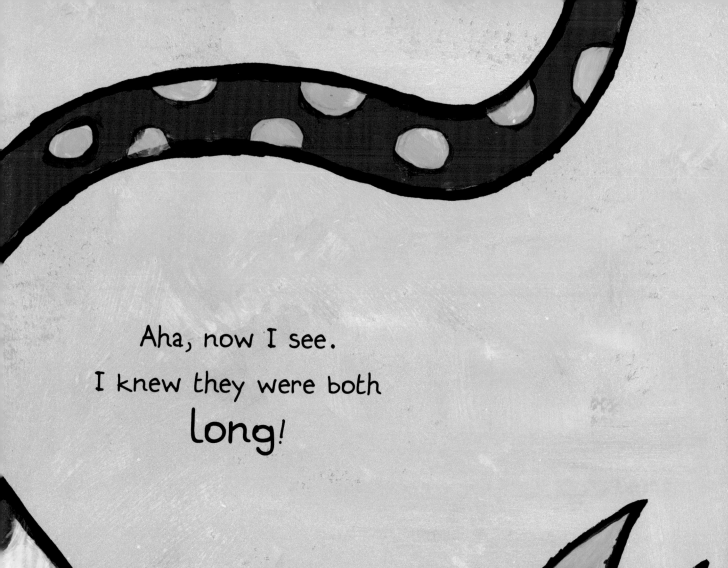

Aha, now I see.
I knew they were both
long!